ANIMAL

Jokes & Riddles

By Jeffrey S. Nelsen

CHECKERBOARD PRESS • NEW YORK

Copyright ©1991 RGA Publishing Group, Inc. All rights reserved.
Published by Checkerboard Press, Inc. ISBN 1-56288-016-0
Printed in the United States of America. 0 9 8 7 6 5 4 3 2 1

How do you make a rabbit stew?

Don't feed him any carrots.

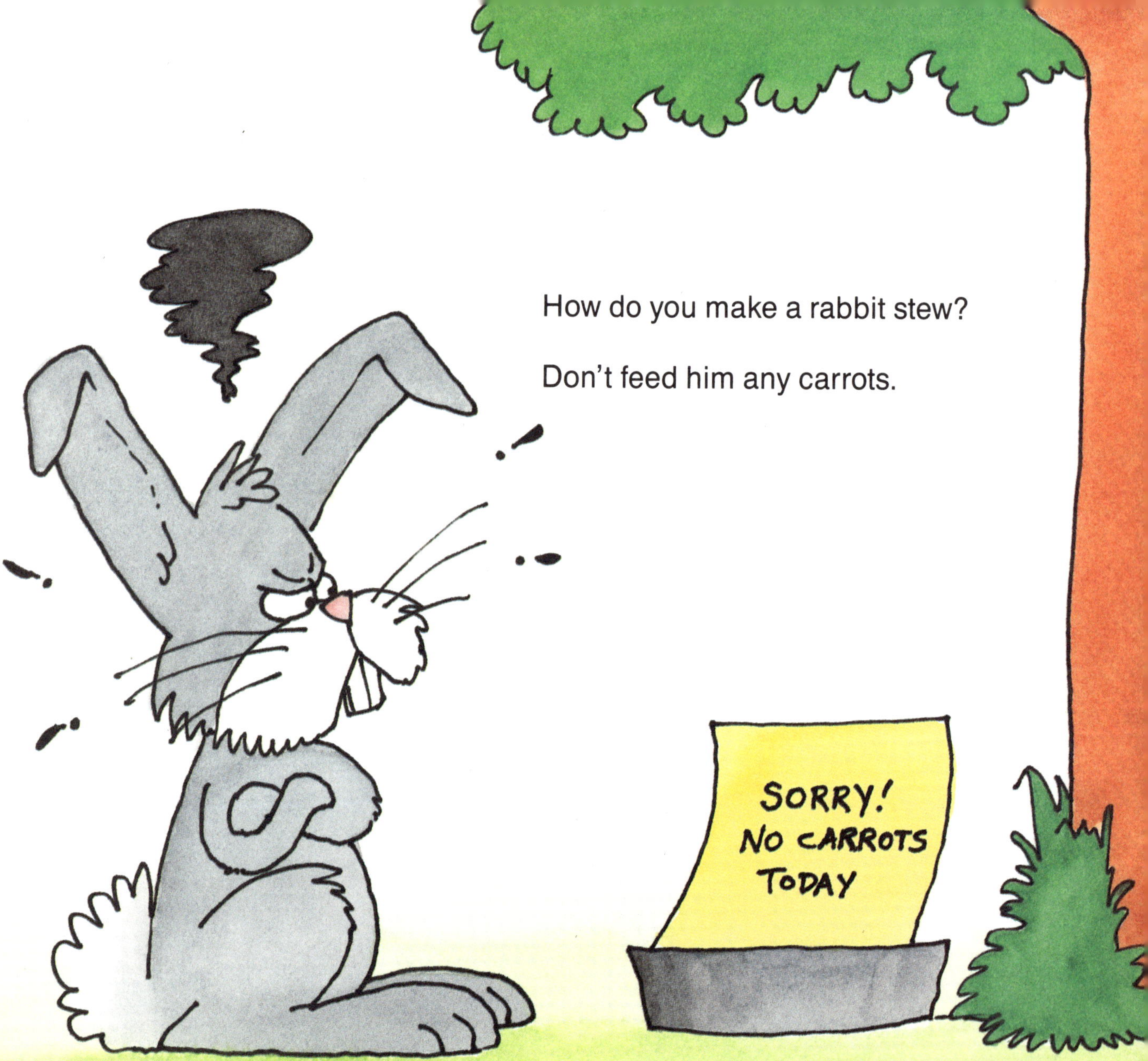
SORRY!
NO CARROTS
TODAY

What do you get when you pour boiling water down a rabbit hole?

Hot, cross bunnies.

Why are skunks so smart?

They have a lot of scents.

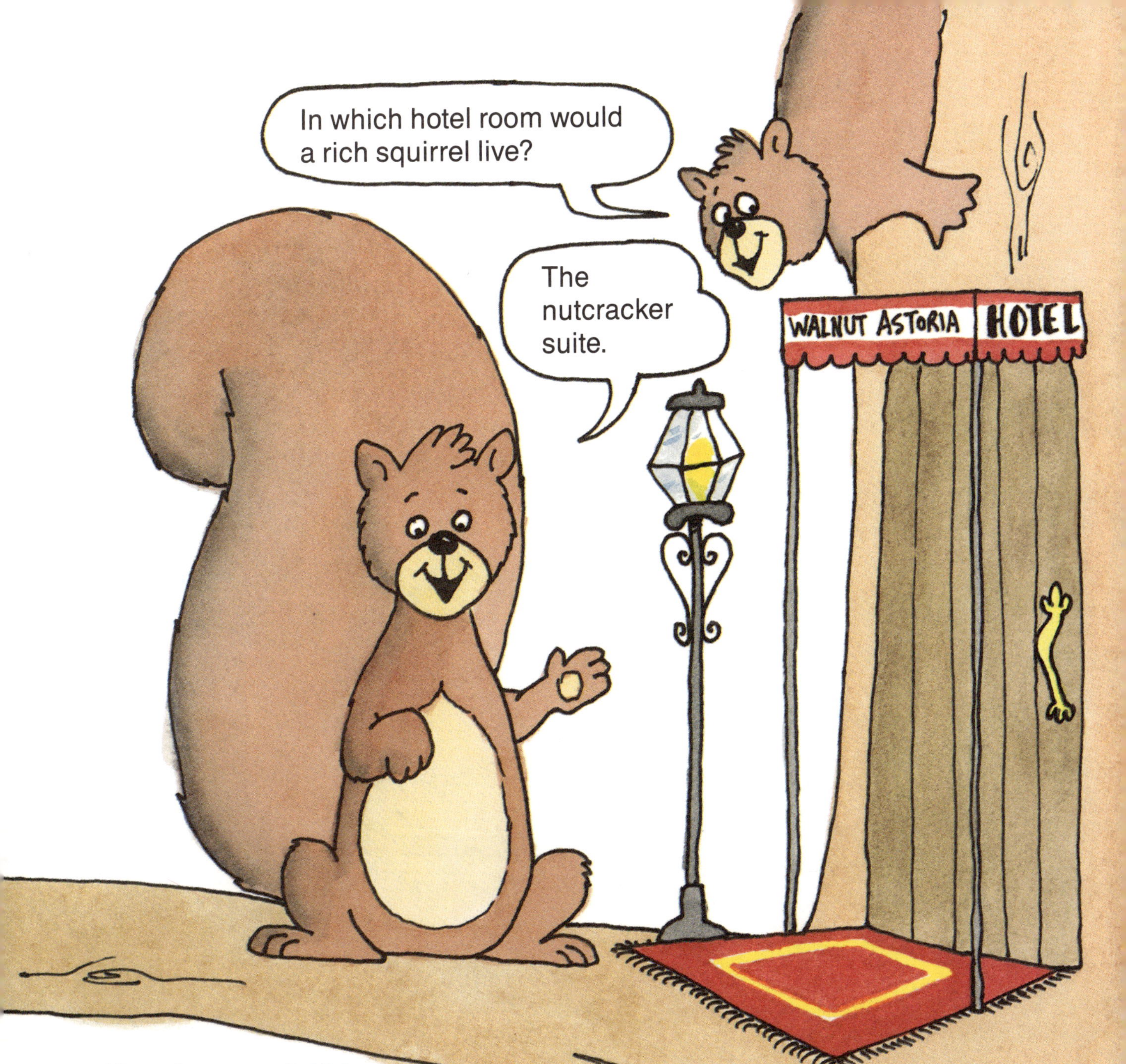
In which hotel room would a rich squirrel live?
The nutcracker suite.
WALNUT ASTORIA
HOTEL

What do you call 20 bunnies moving backward?

A receding hare-line.

Why are some horses so well adjusted?

They were brought up in a stable environment.

What's big and green and likes to bowl?

An alley-gator.

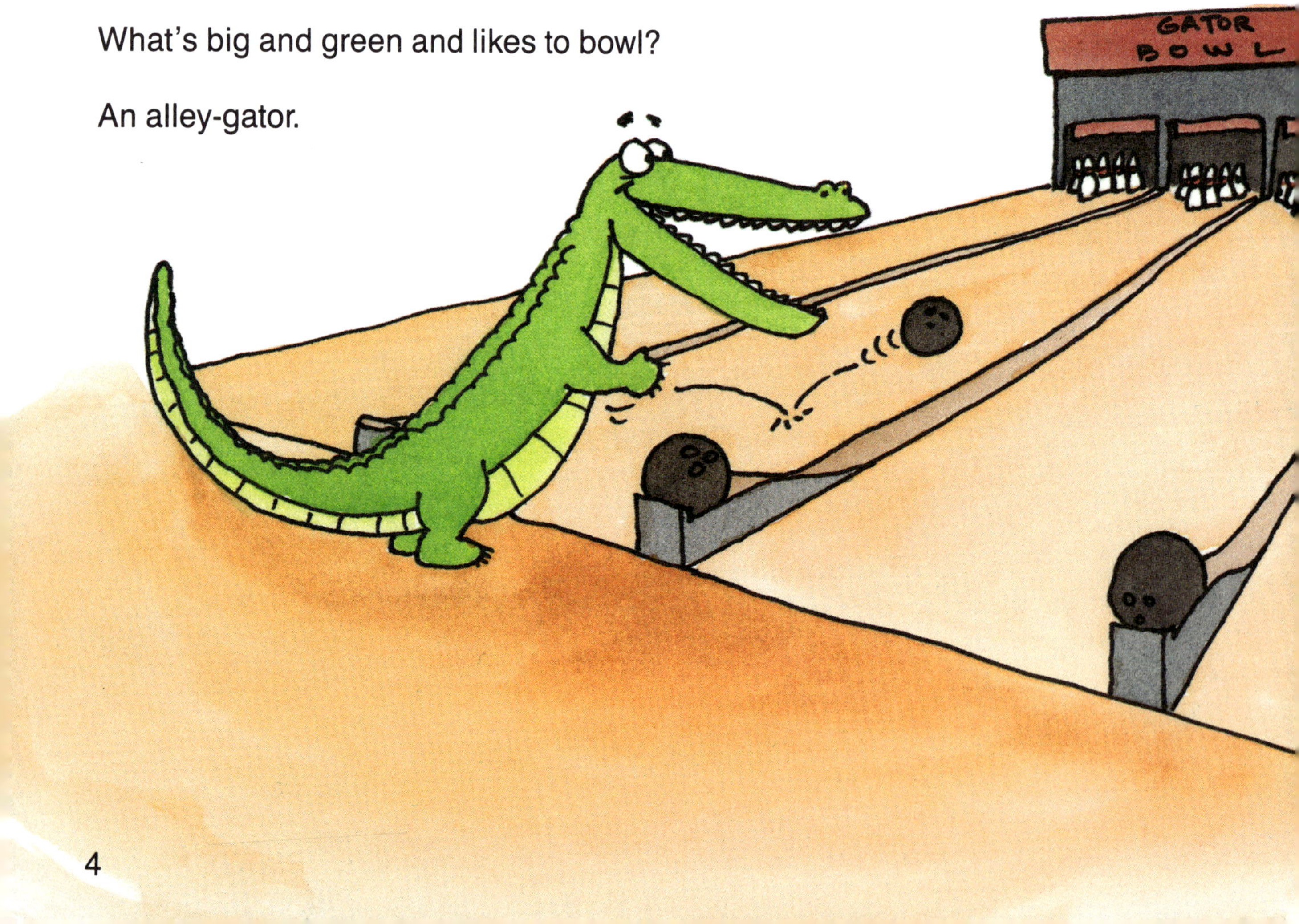
GATOR
BOWL

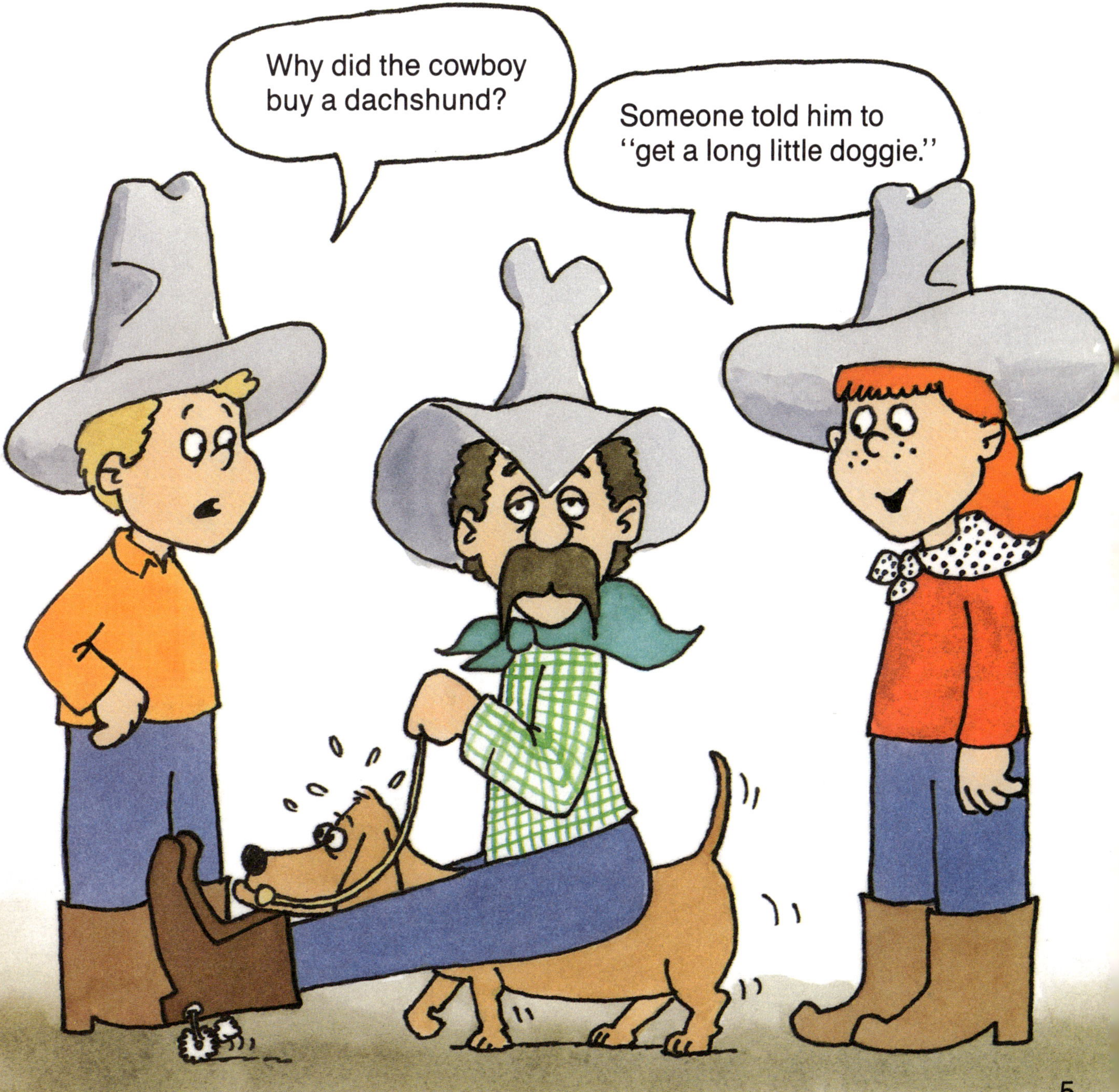
Why did the cowboy buy a dachshund?
Someone told him to "get a long little doggie."

Where do camels go to buy milk?

To a dromedairy.

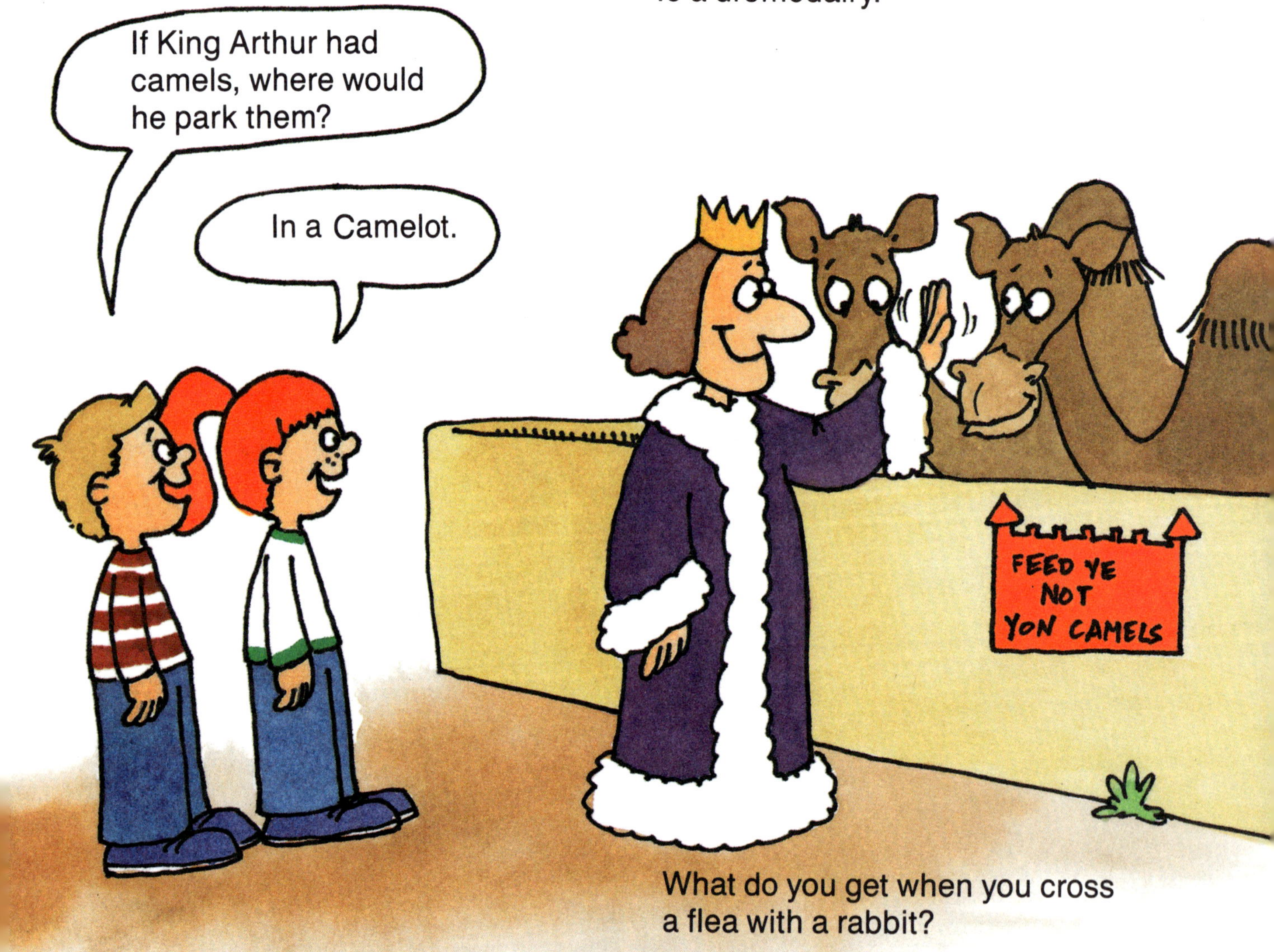
If King Arthur had camels, where would he park them?
In a Camelot.
FEED YE NOT YON CAMELS

What do you get when you cross a flea with a rabbit?

Bugs bunny.

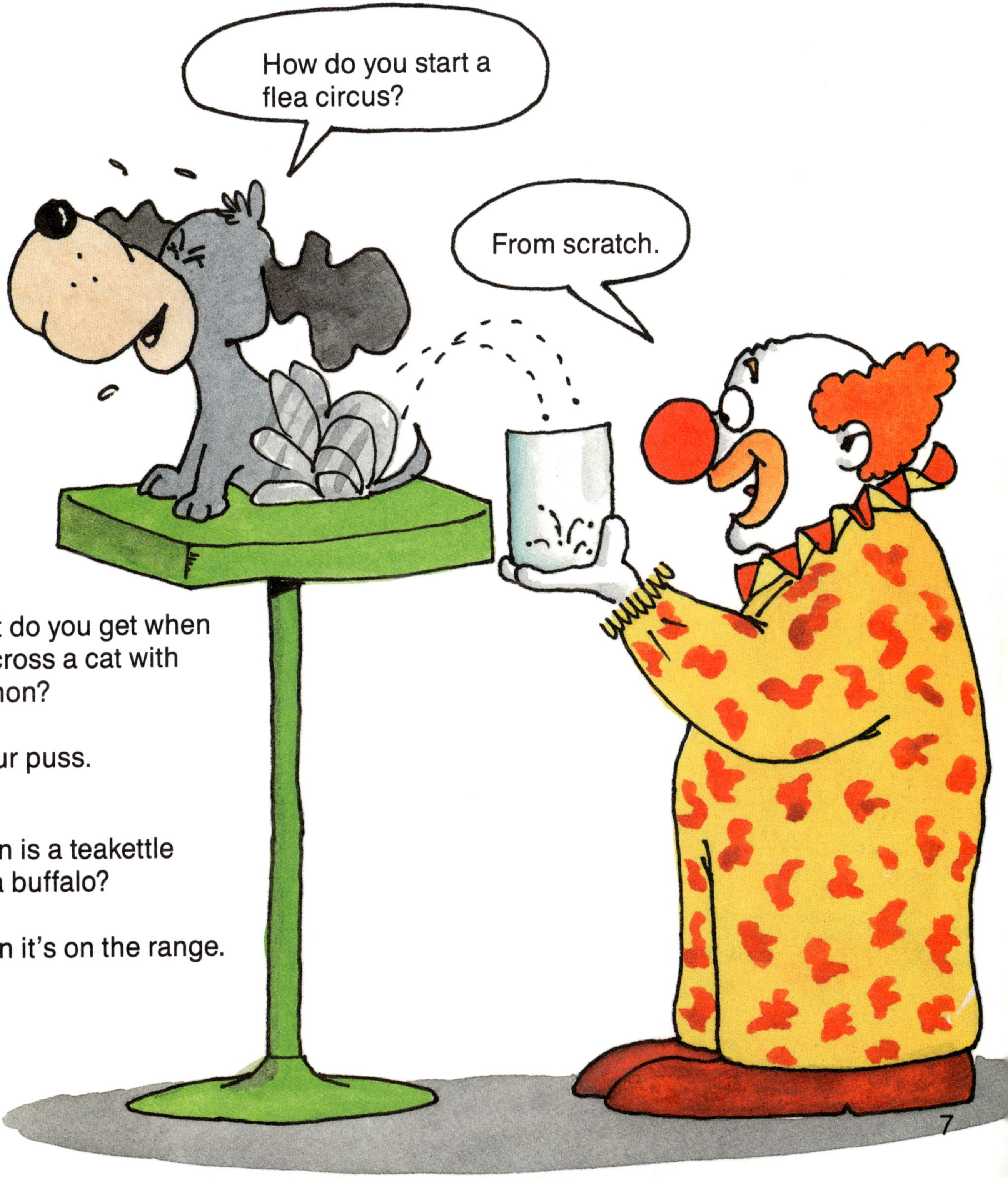
How do you start a flea circus?
From scratch.

What do you get when you cross a cat with a lemon?

A sour puss.

When is a teakettle like a buffalo?

When it's on the range.

Where do you go to buy a dog that goes cheap?

Nowhere. Dogs go "woof-woof." BIRDS go "cheep."

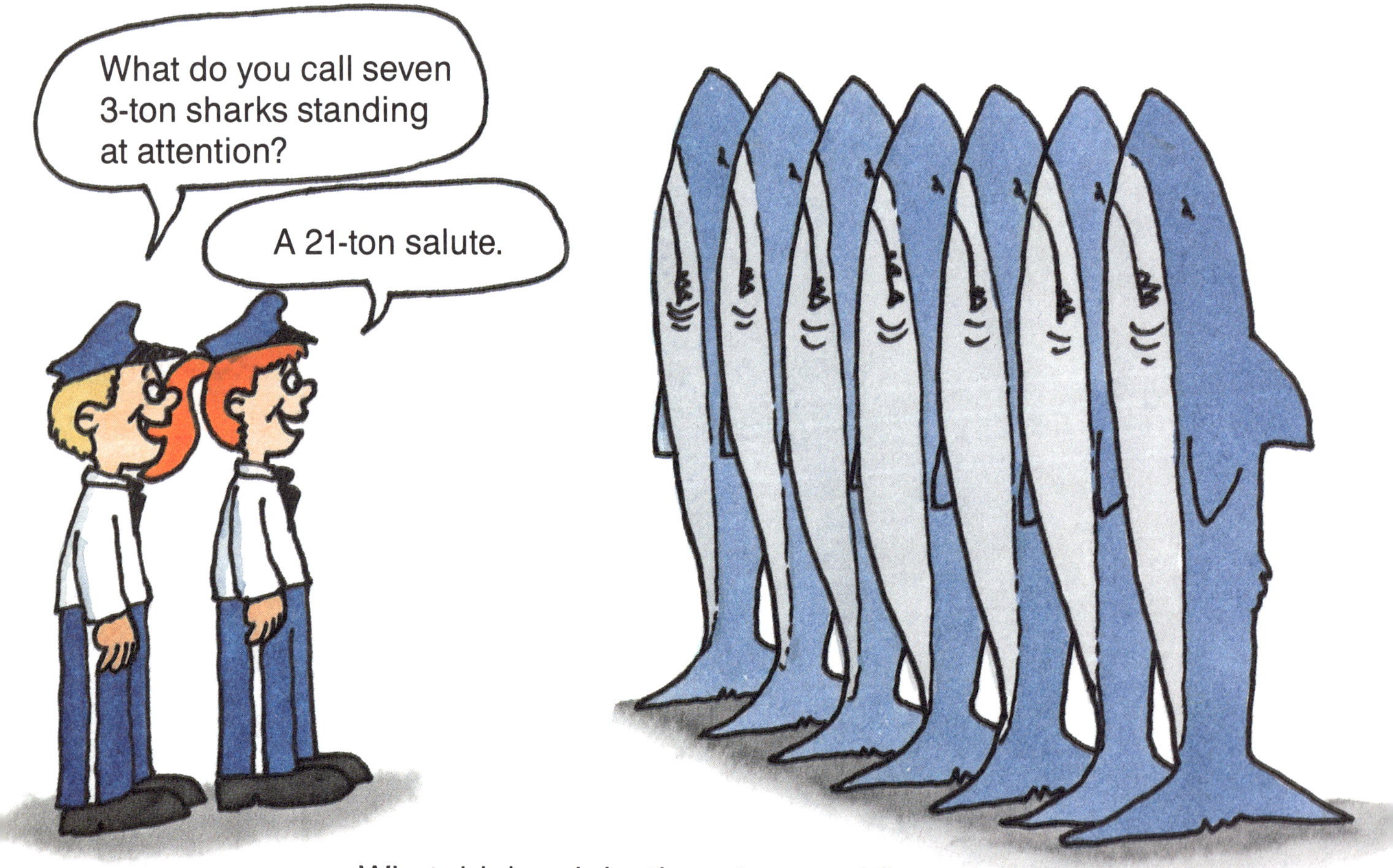
What do you call seven 3-ton sharks standing at attention?
A 21-ton salute.

What drink weighs three tons and fizzes?

Ginger-whale.

What is a bird's favorite kind of fish?

Perch.

What do you call nine people chasing a housefly?

A swat team.

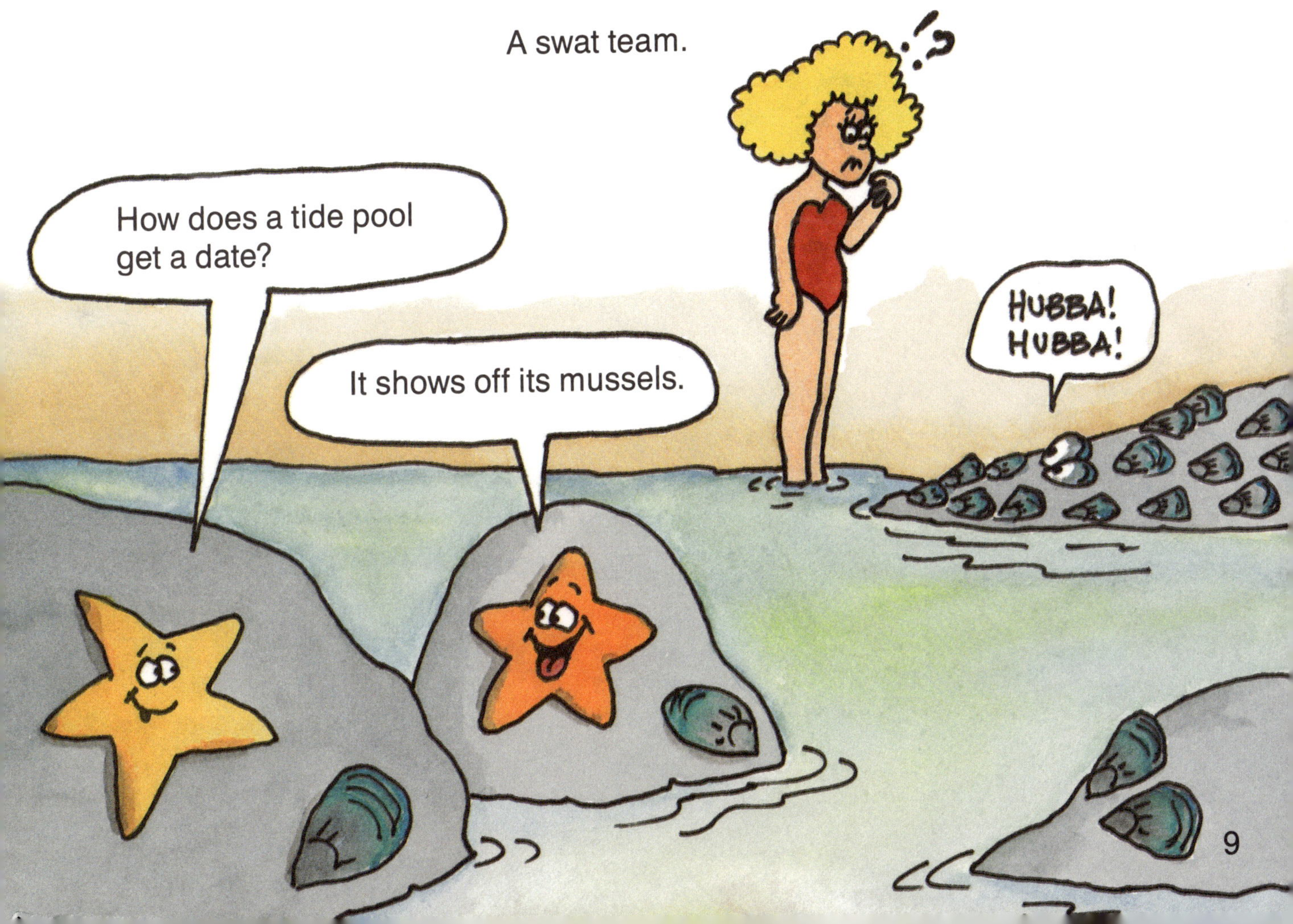

How does a tide pool get a date?
It shows off its mussels.
HUBBA! HUBBA!

How do you lift a duck?

With a quacker-jack.

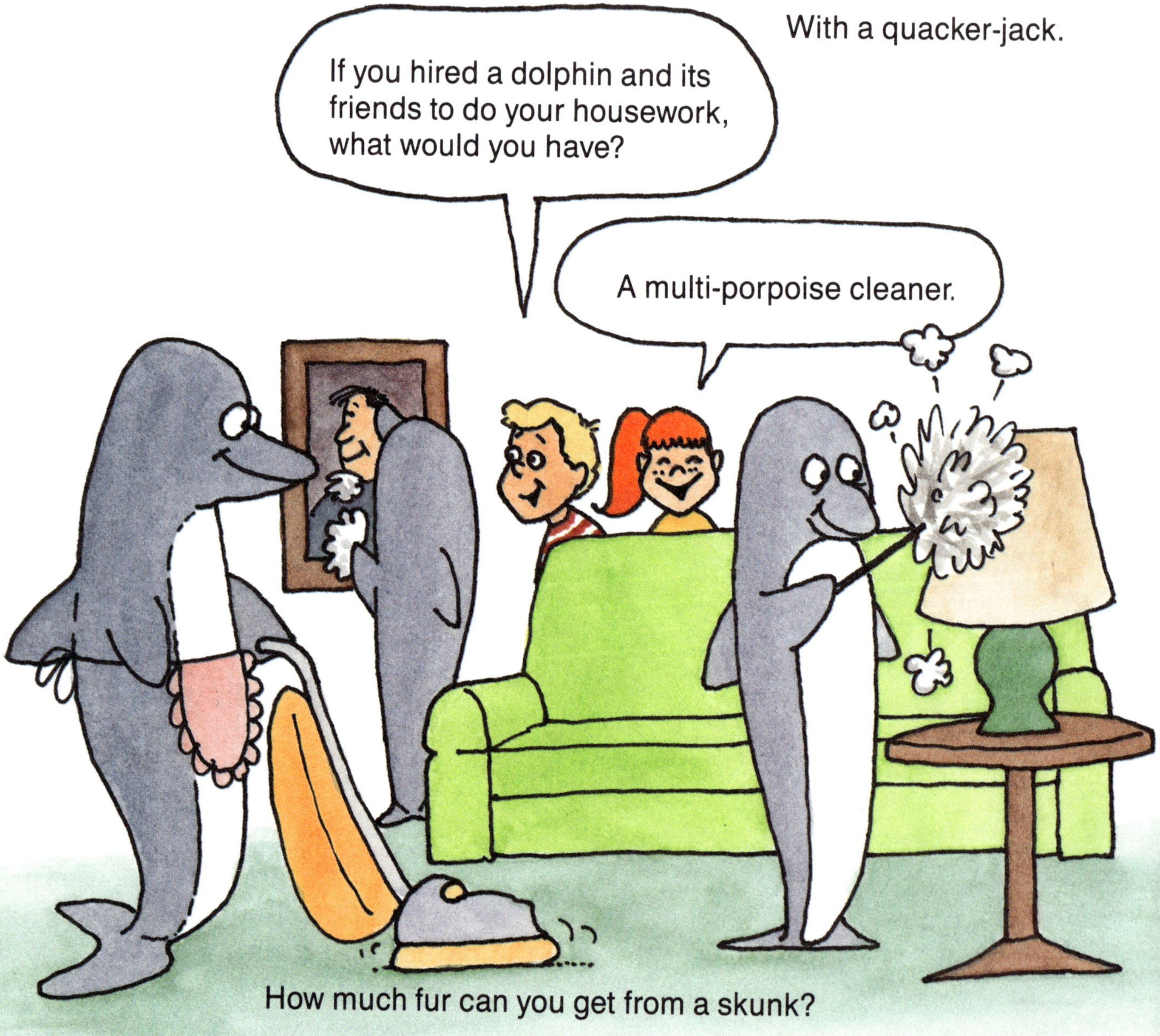

If you hired a dolphin and its friends to do your housework, what would you have?
A multi-porpoise cleaner.

How much fur can you get from a skunk?

Just as fur as you can.

What do you call someone who catches ducks, geese, and pelicans?

A bill collector.

Why don't birds ever listen to each other?

Because their talk is cheep.

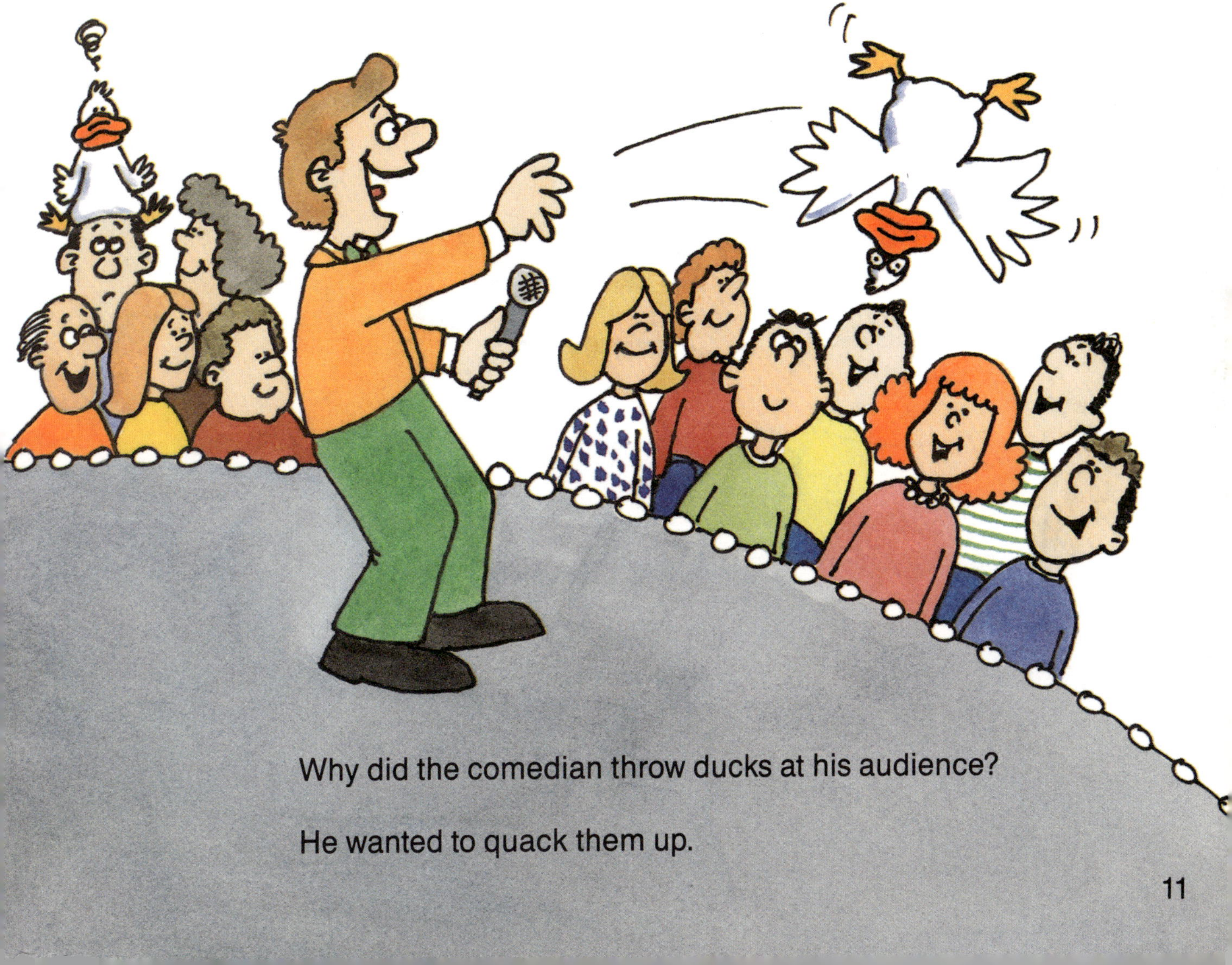

Why did the comedian throw ducks at his audience?

He wanted to quack them up.

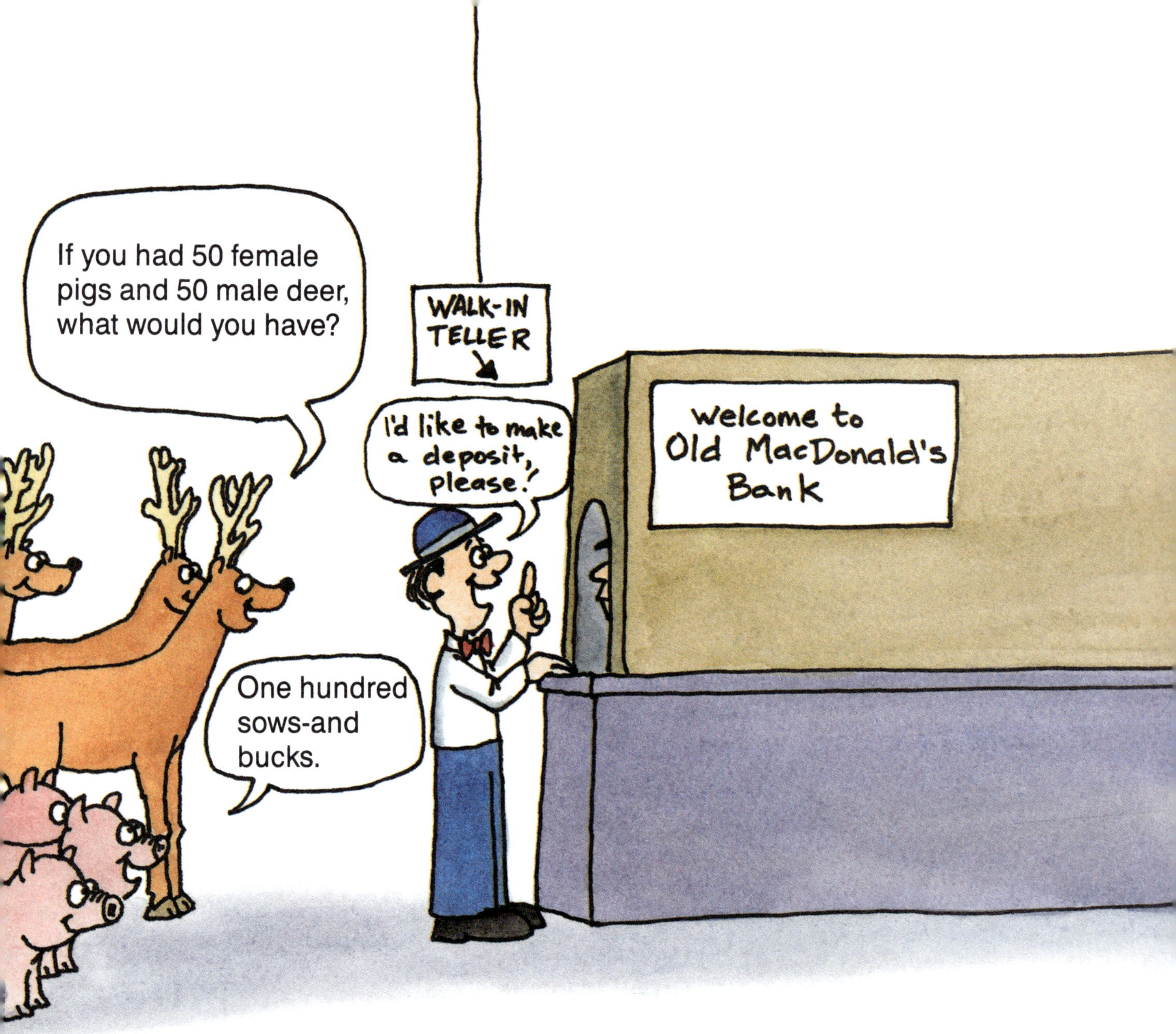
If you had 50 female pigs and 50 male deer, what would you have?
WALK-IN TELLER
I'd like to make a deposit, please.
Welcome to Old MacDonald's Bank
One hundred sows-and bucks.

How are deer hunters and responsible people alike?

Neither one of them likes to pass a buck.

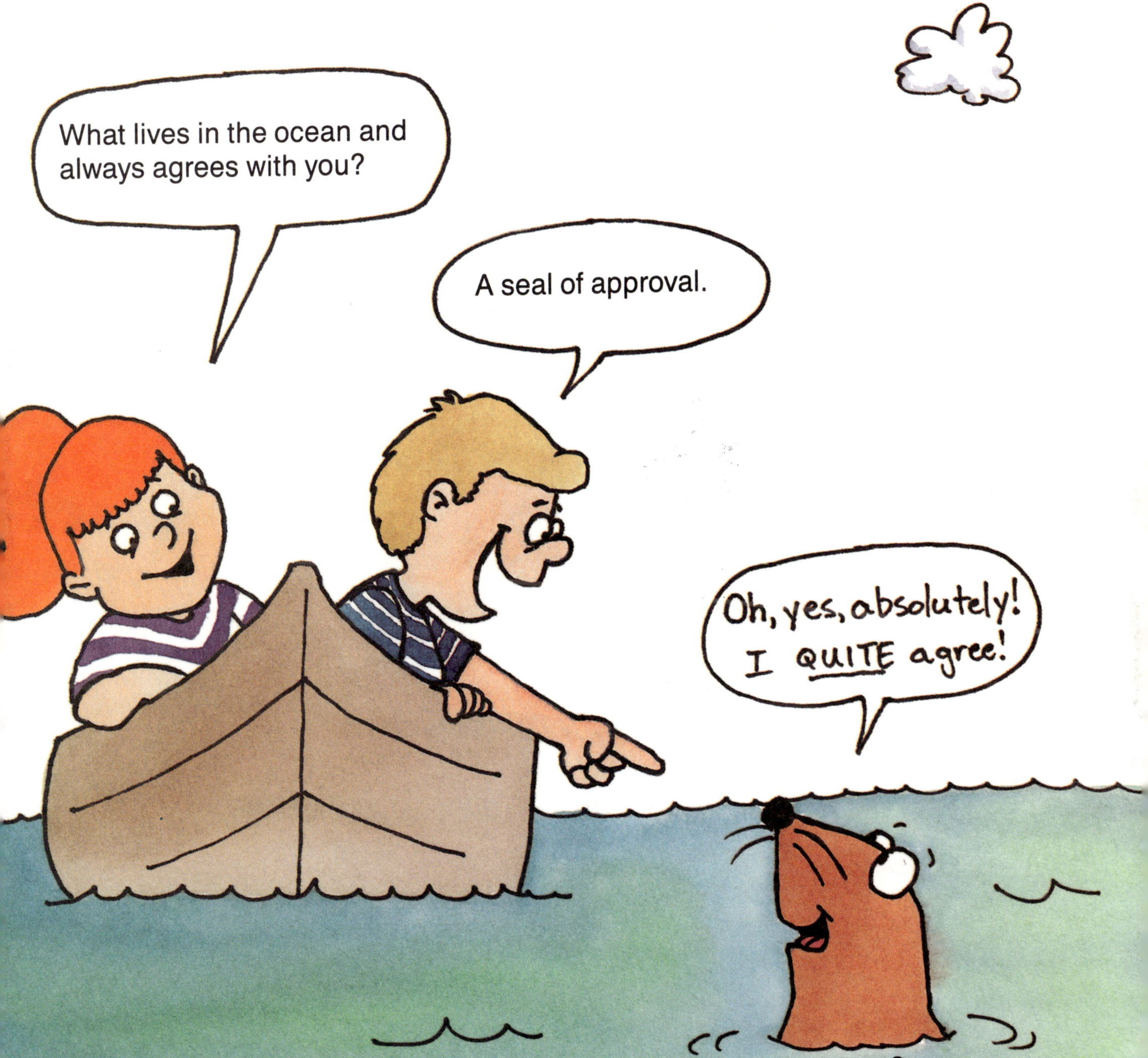
What lives in the ocean and always agrees with you?
A seal of approval.
Oh, yes, absolutely! I QUITE agree!

What happens before a baby goose grows up?

It grows down.

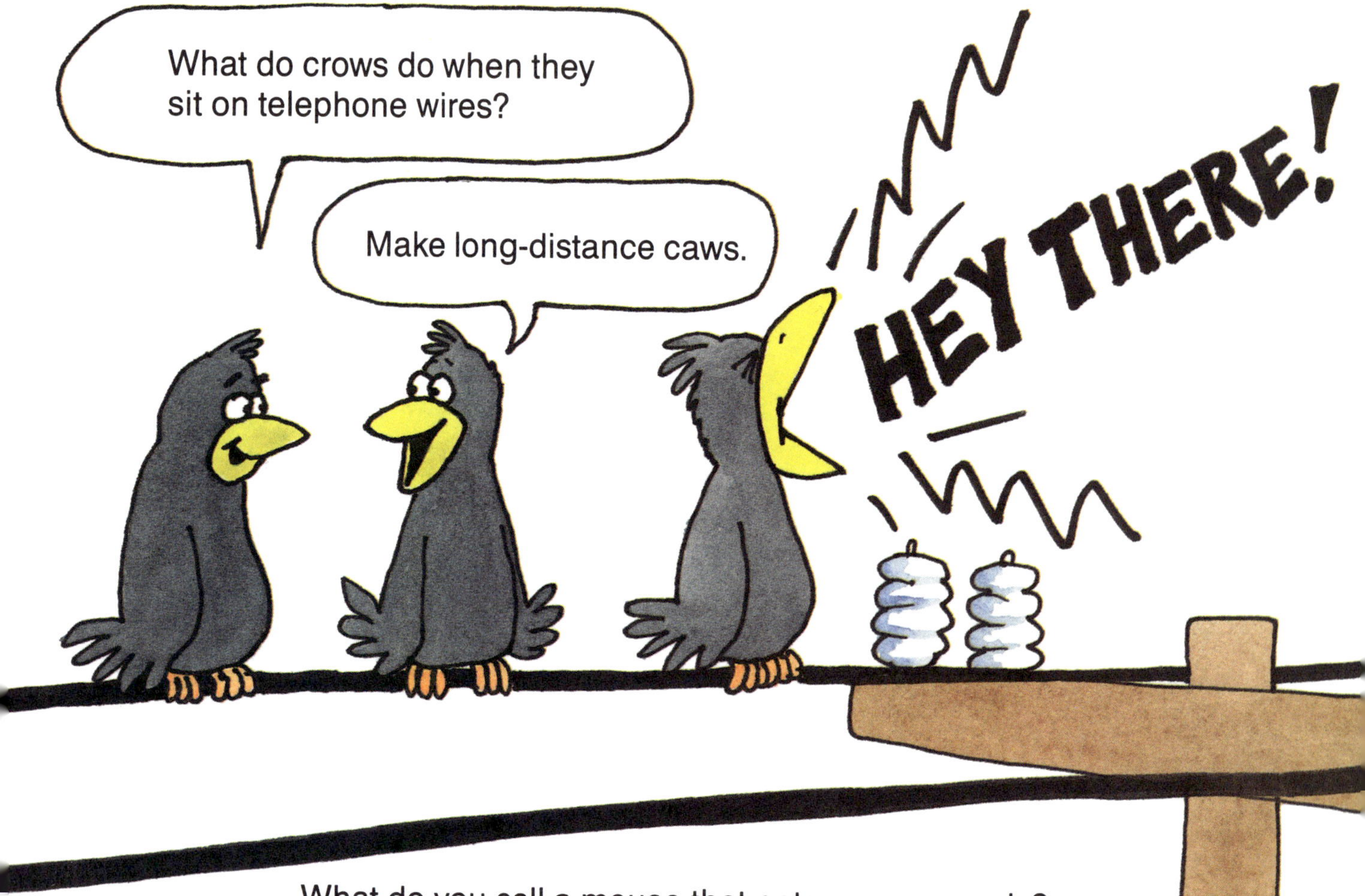
What do crows do when they sit on telephone wires?
Make long-distance caws.
HEY THERE!

What do you call a mouse that eats orange seeds?

A pip-squeak.

What has four legs and goes "oom-oom"?

A cow walking backward.

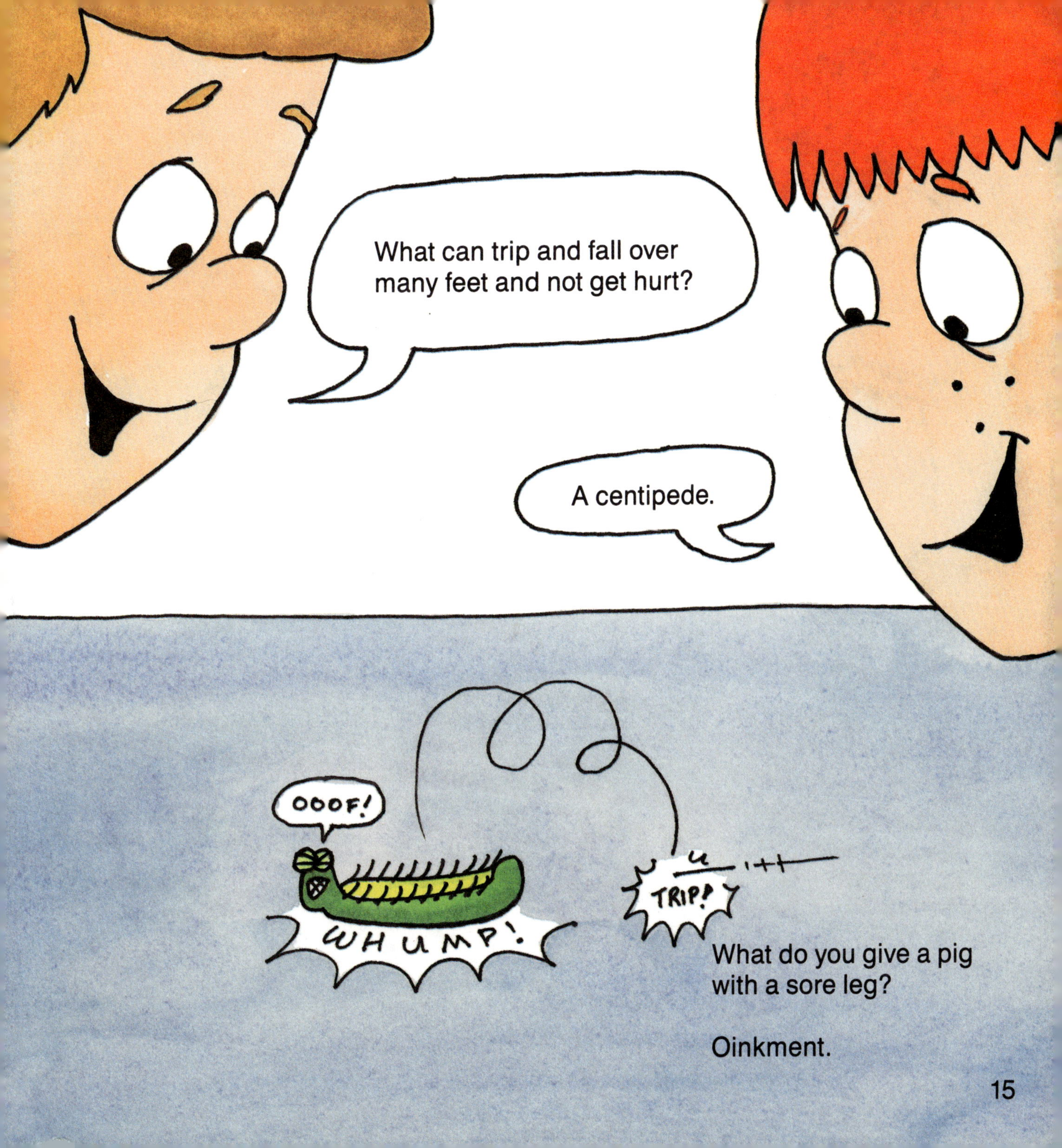
What can trip and fall over many feet and not get hurt?
A centipede.
OOOF!
TRIP!
WHUMP!

What do you give a pig
with a sore leg?

Oinkment.

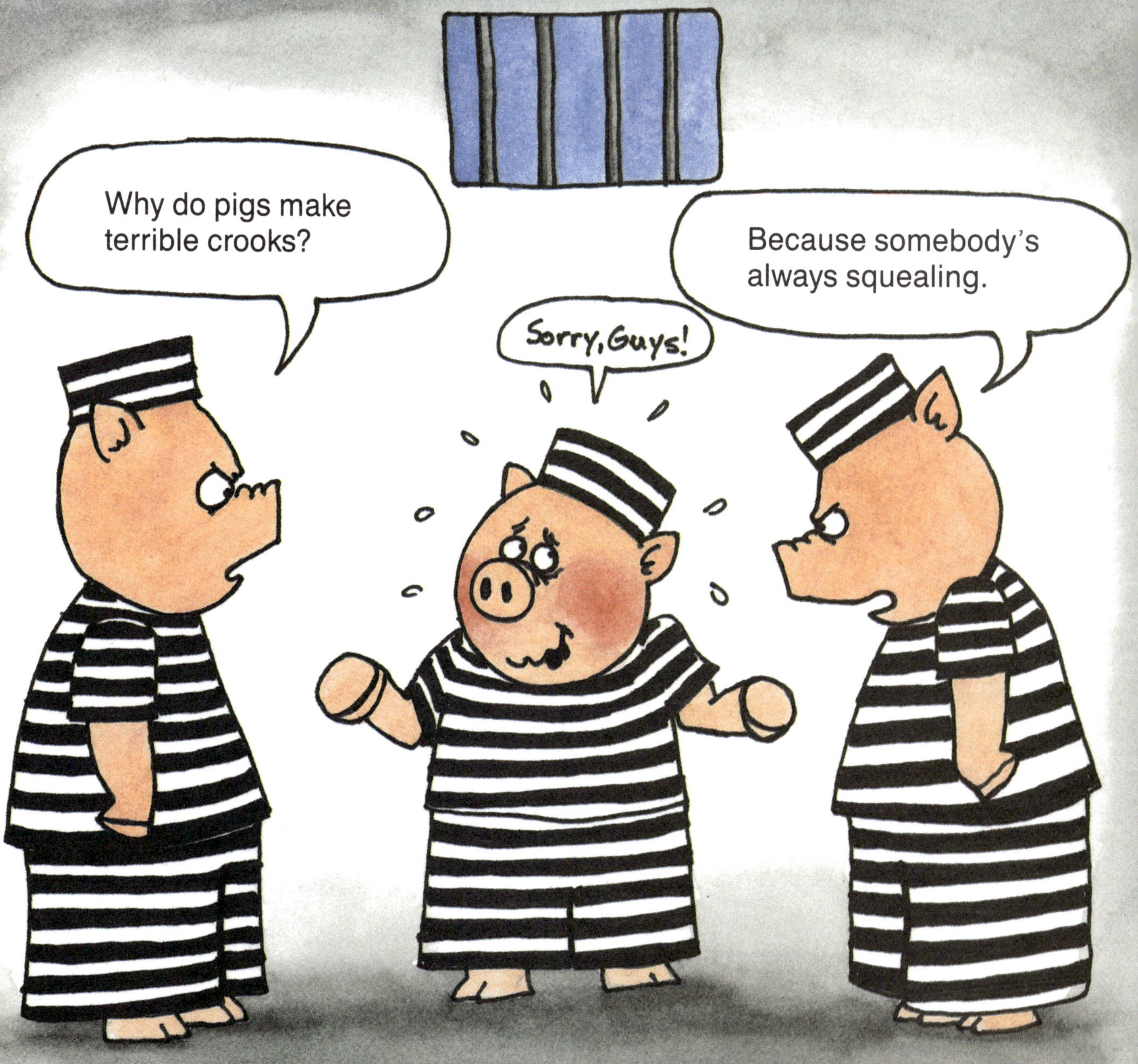
Why do pigs make terrible crooks?
Sorry, Guys!
Because somebody's always squealing.

What do you call a pig farmer who has lost all his pigs?

Disgruntled.

Why was the fish turned down by the army?

It failed the herring test.

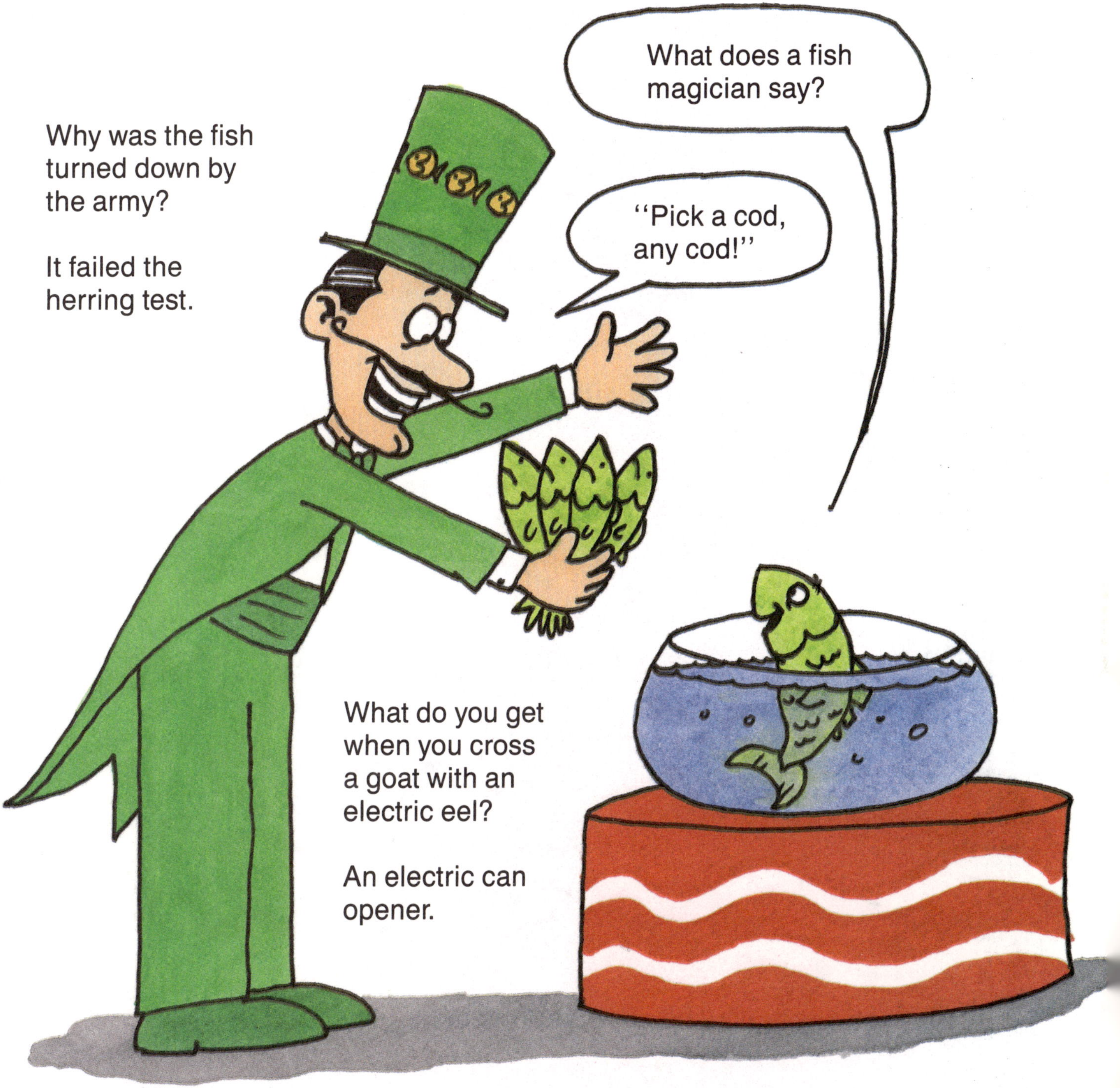
What does a fish magician say?
"Pick a cod, any cod!"

What do you get when you cross a goat with an electric eel?

An electric can opener.

What do you call a poodle in a tub?

A shampoodle.

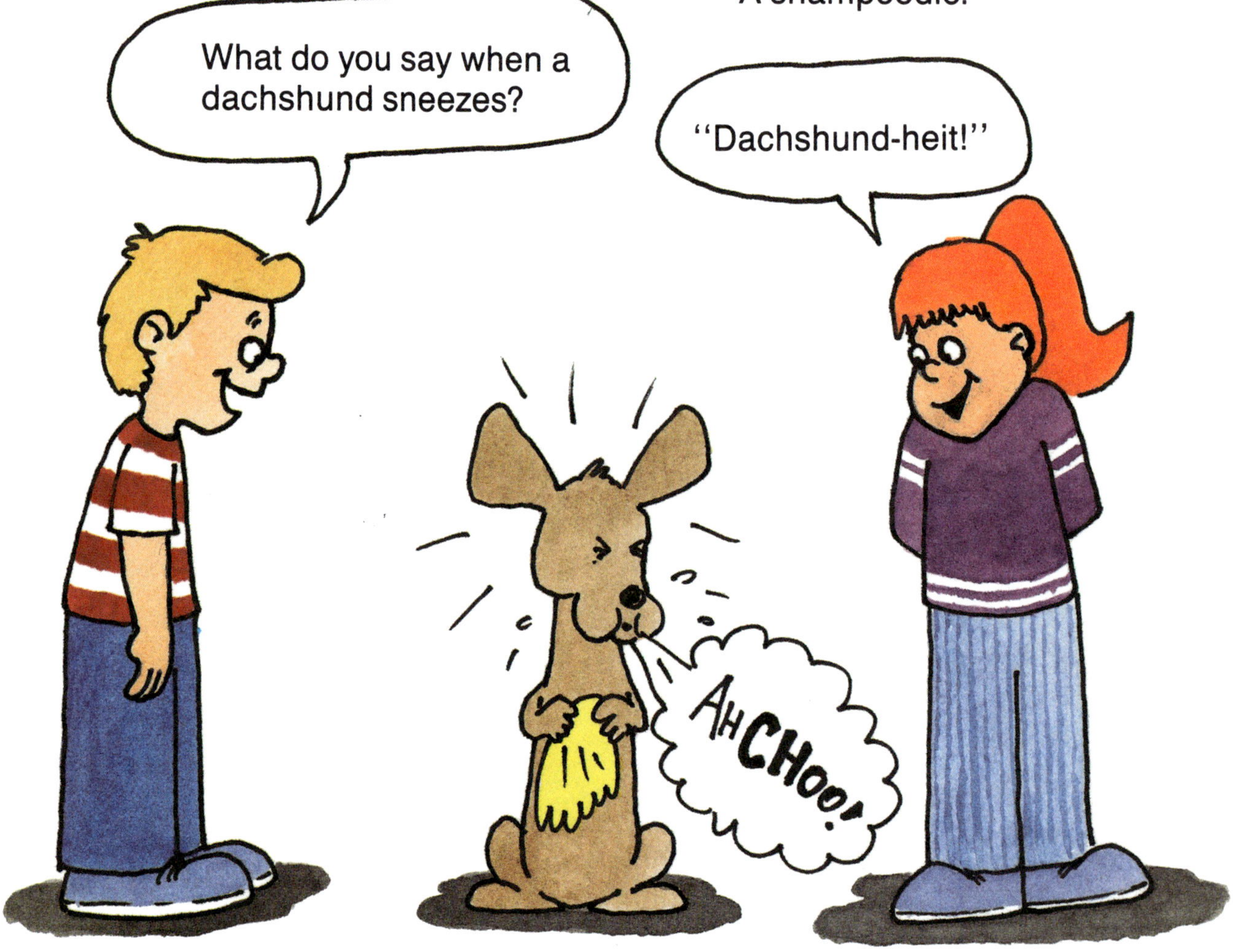
What do you say when a dachshund sneezes?
"Dachshund-heit!"
AH CHOO!

Why did the watchdog run around in circles?

To wind itself up.

What do you call a dog that's always doing tricks?

A show-arf.

What comic strip do sheep like to read?

Mutton Jeff.

Why don't schools of fish ever graduate?

Because they're always below C level.

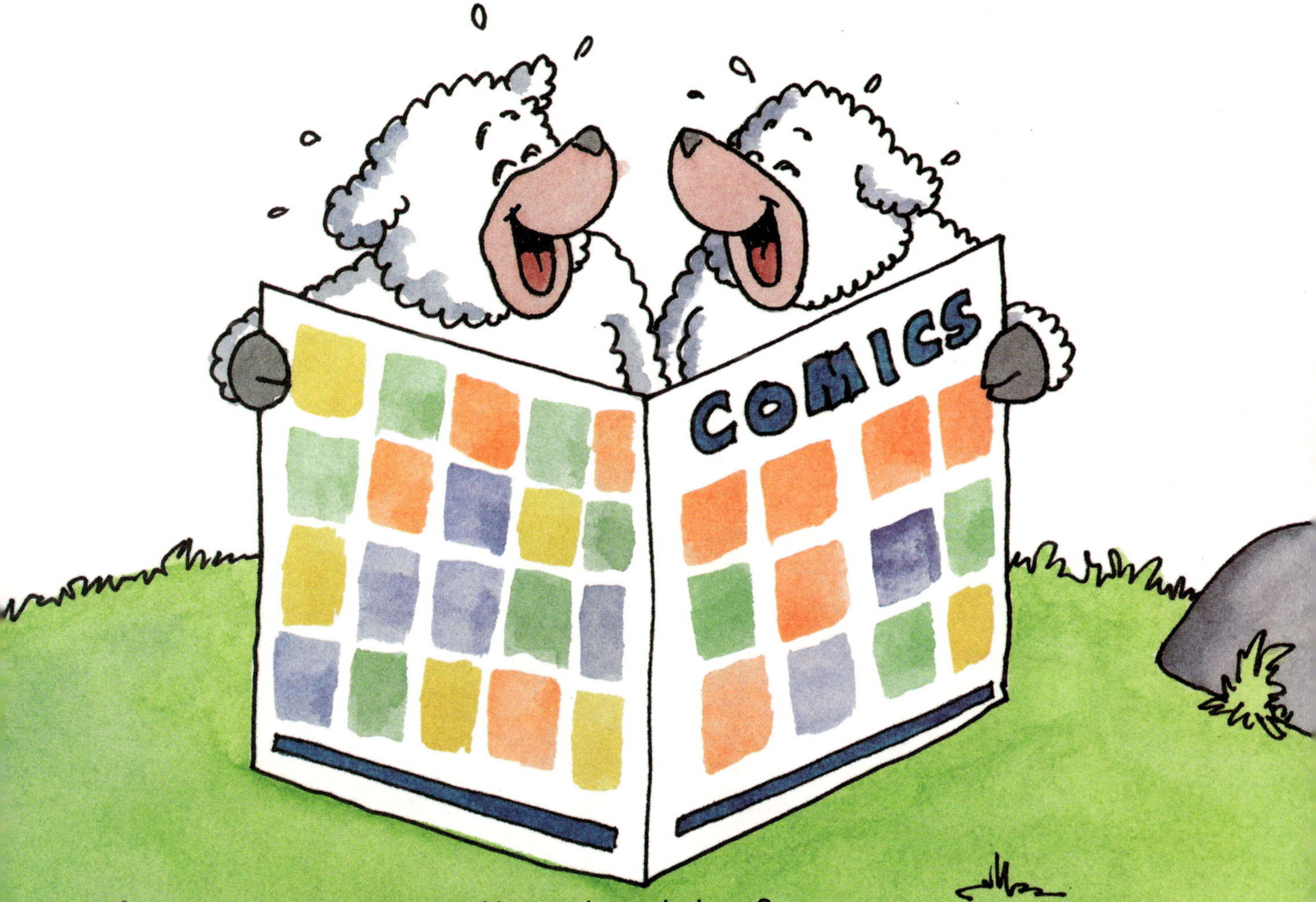
COMICS

What kind of horse has six legs?

They all do. They have forelegs in front and two in back.

What's a name for a dumb dog?

Fi-dodo.

What does a dog do
that a man steps in?

Pants.

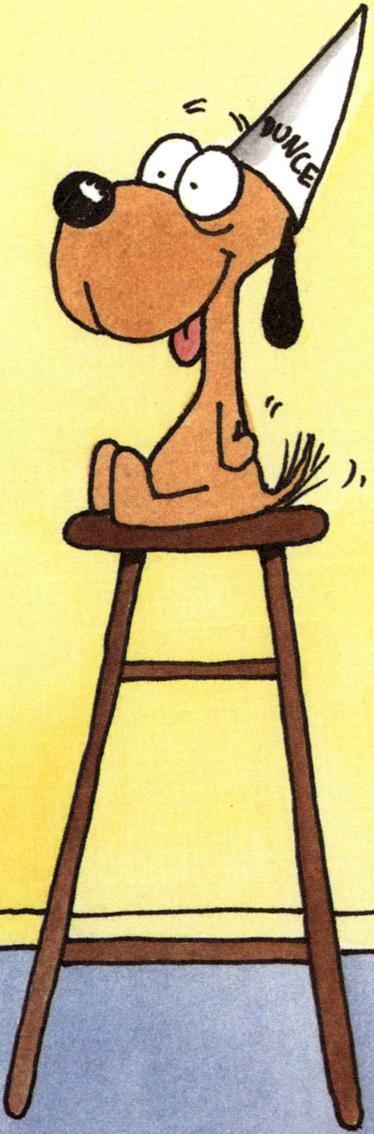
DUNCE

Does a dog wear more
clothes in winter or
in summer?

Summer. In winter
it wears a coat, but
in summer a dog wears
a coat and pants.

What's the opposite
of a hot dog?

A pupsicle.

What do you get when
an orangutan punches
you in the eye?

A monkey shiner.

What do you call a bone that a dog ran 10 miles to retrieve?

Far-fetched.

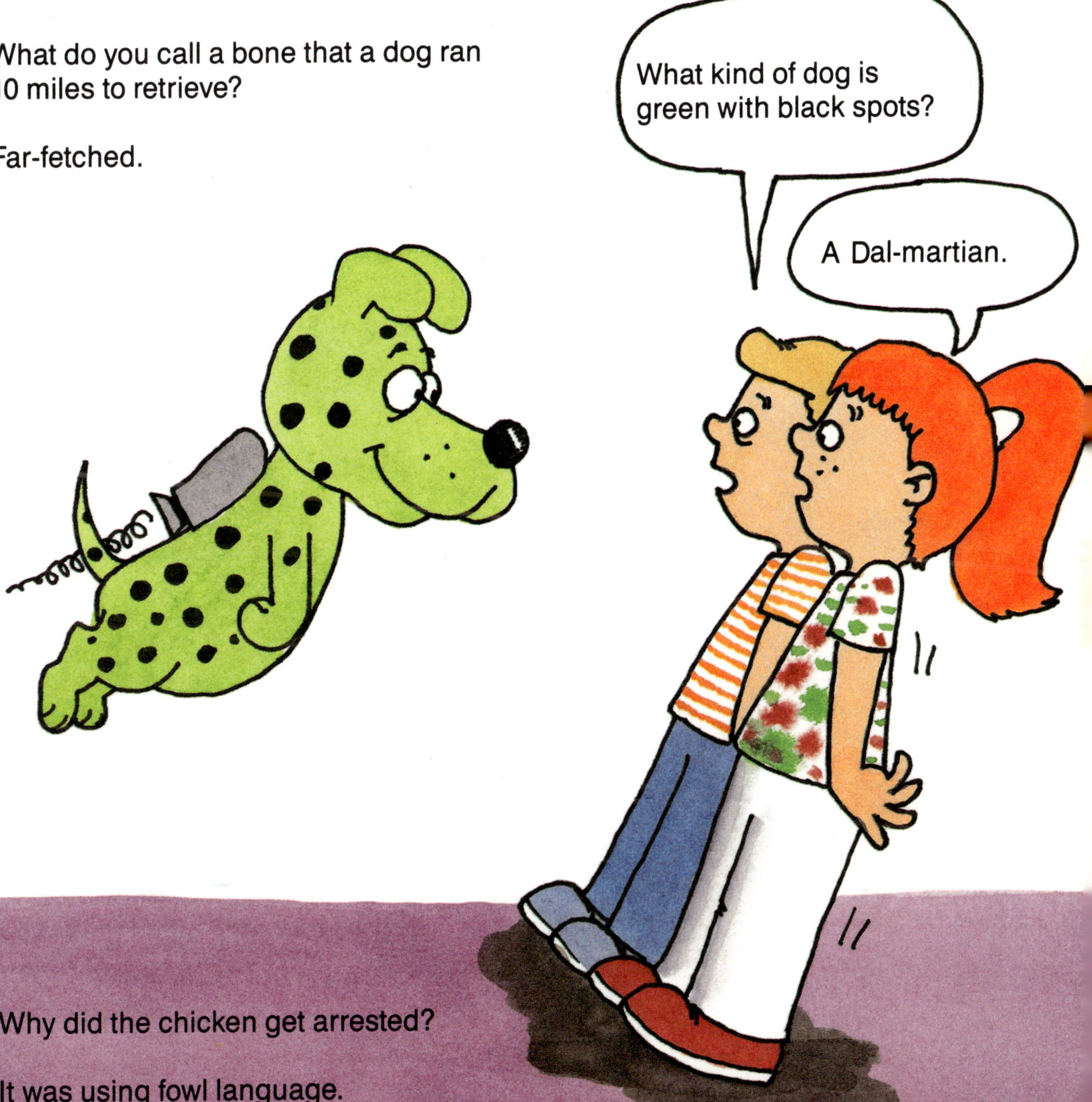
What kind of dog is green with black spots?
A Dal-martian.

Why did the chicken get arrested?

It was using fowl language.

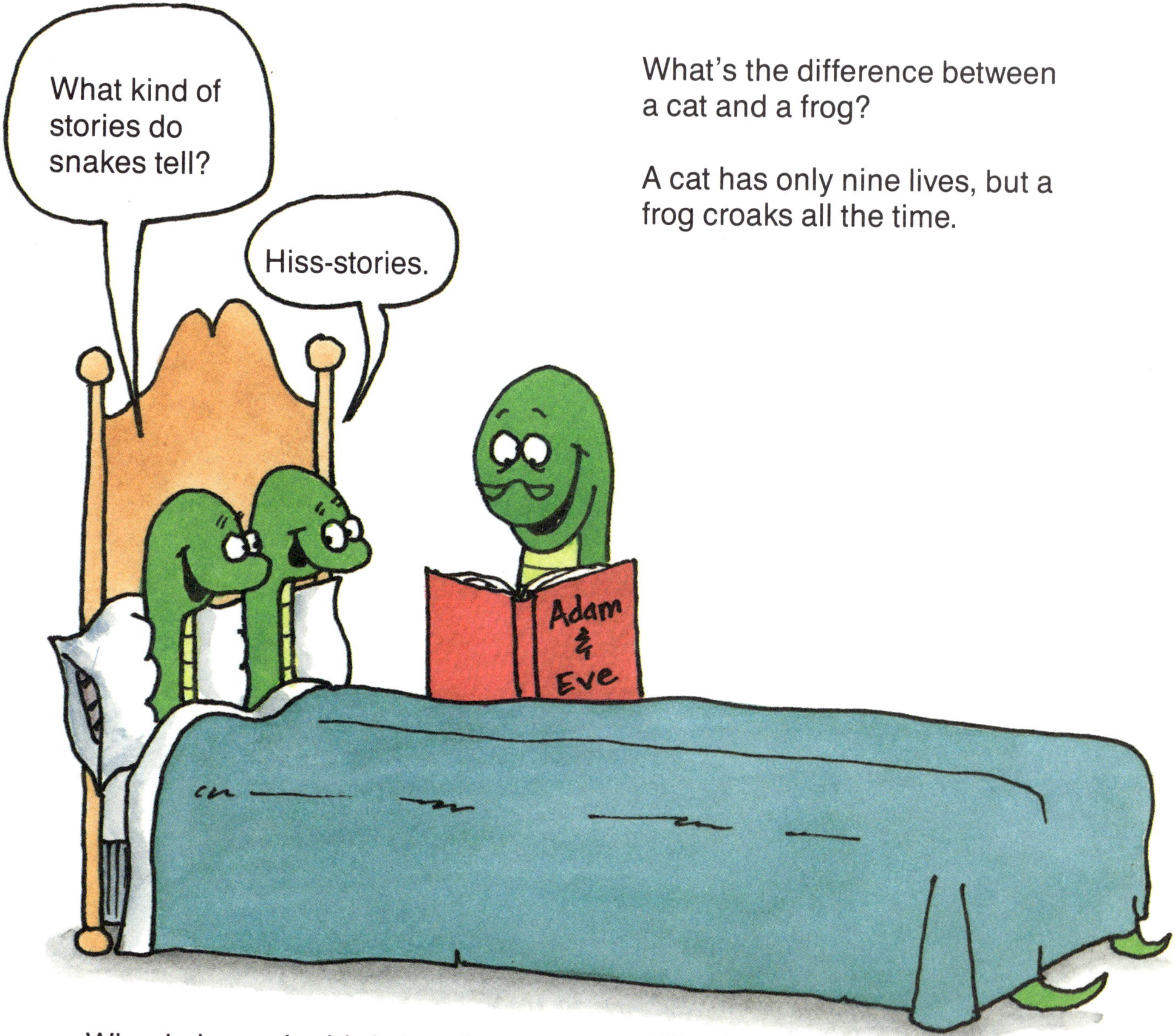
What kind of stories do snakes tell?
Hiss-stories.
Adam & Eve

What's the difference between a cat and a frog?

A cat has only nine lives, but a frog croaks all the time.

Why do hummingbirds hum?

They don't know how to yodel.

What's a cow's favorite song?

"Mooin' River."

How do you know when it's raining cats and dogs?

When you step into a poodle.

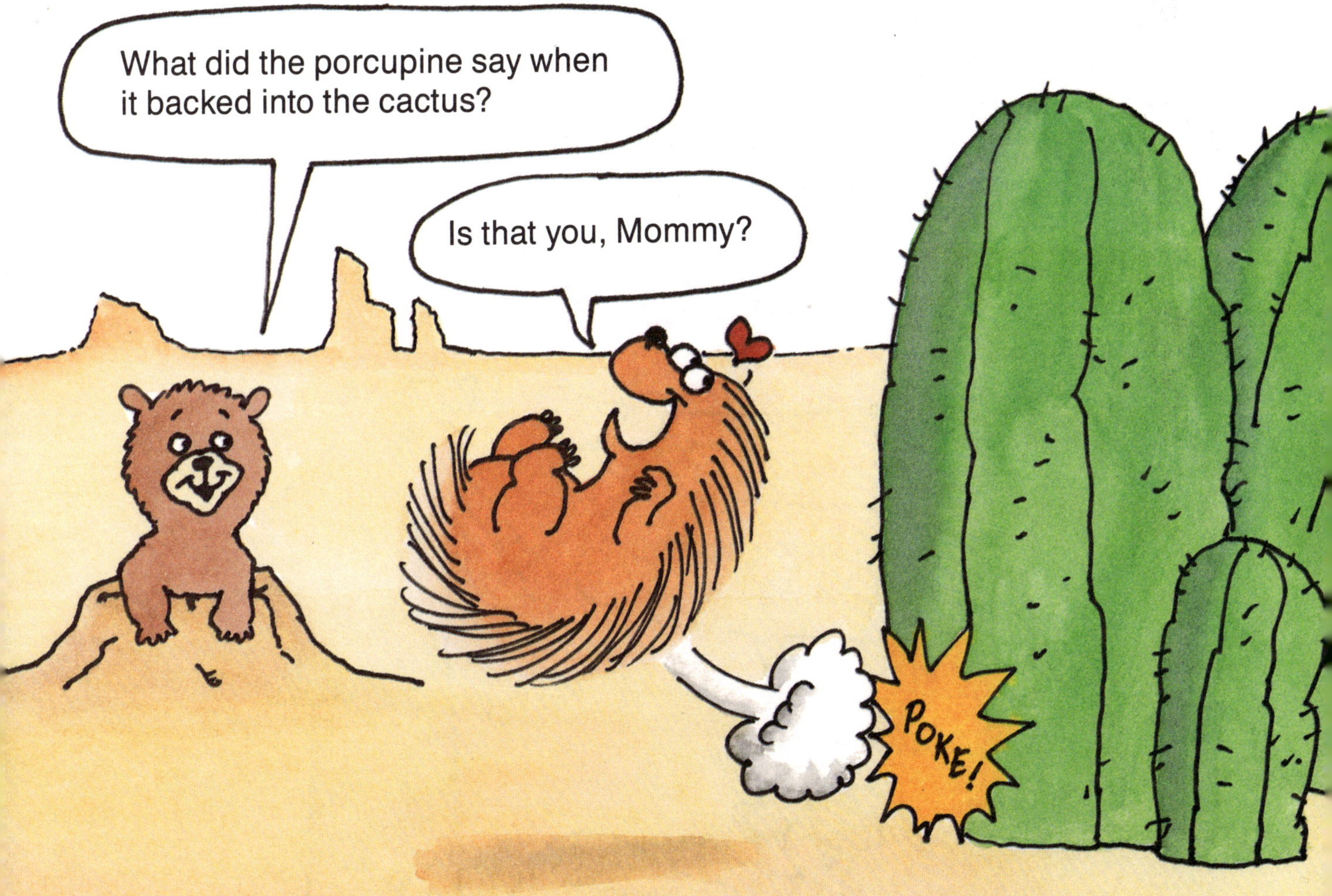
What did the porcupine say when it backed into the cactus?
Is that you, Mommy?
POKE!

What do police officers use to arrest a pig?

Hamcuffs.

What flies through the air and has buck teeth?

A frisbeaver.

What's a cat's favorite holiday?

Christmouse.

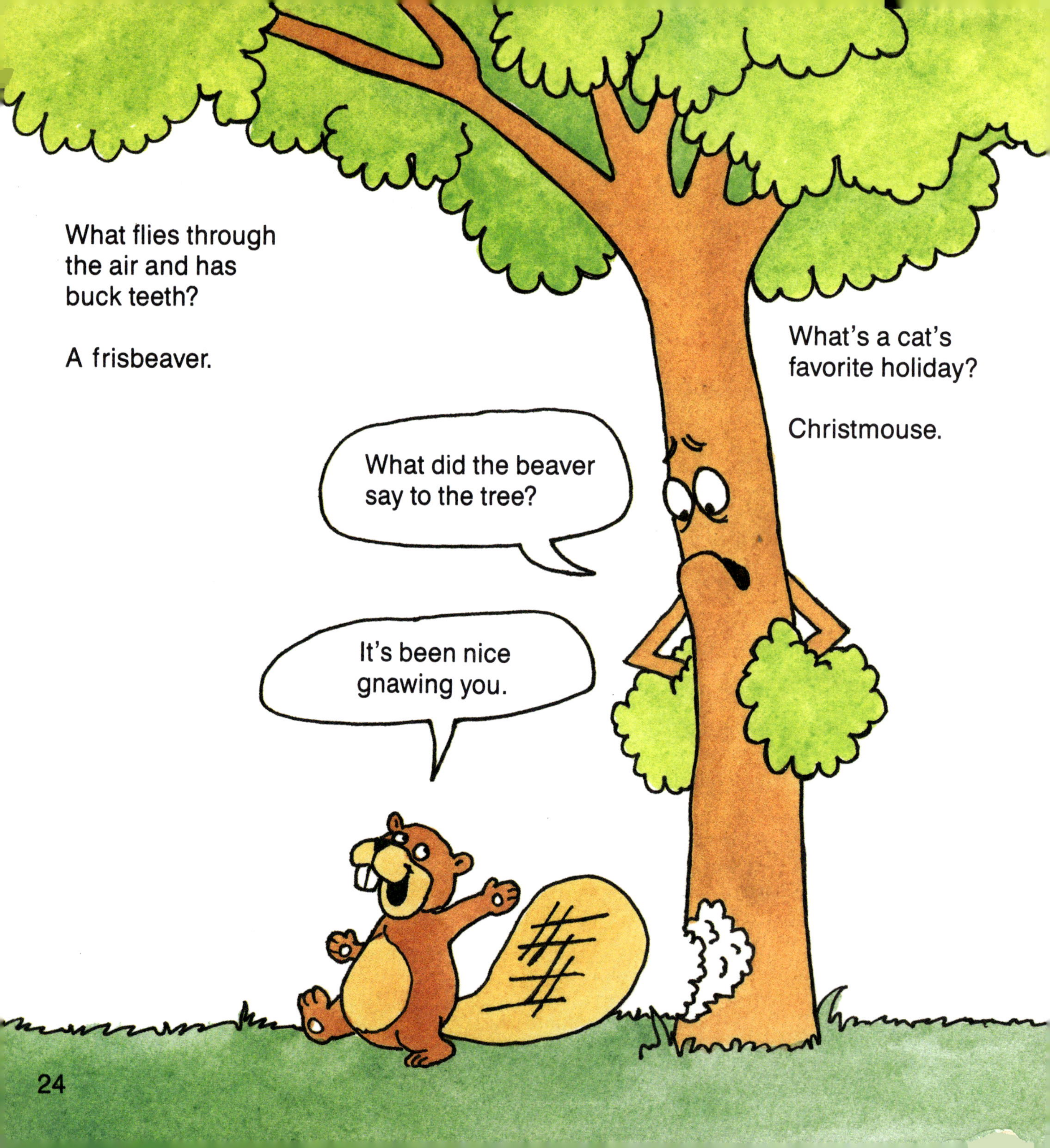
What did the beaver say to the tree?
It's been nice gnawing you.